Princess Mirror-Belle

and Prince Precious Paws

Books by Julia Donaldson

★ JULIA DONALDSON ★

Princess Mirror-Belle

and Prince Precious Paws

Illustrated by
✳ LYDIA MONKS ✳

MACMILLAN CHILDREN'S BOOKS

These stories first published 2005 in *Princess Mirror-Belle and the Magic Shoes* by
Macmillan Children's Books

This edition published 2017 by Macmillan Children's Books
an imprint of Pan Macmillan
20 New Wharf Road, London N1 9RR
Associated companies throughout the world
www.panmacmillan.com

ISBN 978-1-5098-8025-6

Text copyright © Julia Donaldson 2005
Illustrations copyright © Lydia Monks 2005, 2015

1 3 5 7 9 8 6 4 2

A CIP catalogue record for this book is available from
the British Library.

Printed and bound by CPI Group (UK) Ltd, Croydon CR0 4YY

For Millie and Olly

Contents

Chapter One

Prince Precious Paws

"Good, Splodge. Good dog."

For the twentieth time that morning, Ellen picked up the boring-looking stick which lay at her feet. Splodge was gazing up at her with what she called his "Again" look.

"All right, then." Ellen strolled a little way along the lakeside path and then

1

hurled the stick as hard as she could. It landed with a splash in the lake.

In a brown-and-white flash, Splodge was at the water's edge. But there he stopped.

"Go on, Splodge – get it!"

Ellen felt like jumping in herself, the lake looked so cool and inviting under the hot blue sky. But Splodge seemed to have forgotten all about the stick. He was staring into the rippled water and barking. What had he seen? Ellen looked down too. The ripples were clearing now, but all she could see was Splodge's reflection – and her own.

Suddenly the water at their feet started to churn, whirling and splashing as if some huge fish were writhing about in it.

The next second another brown-and-white dog was shaking itself all over Ellen. Splodge barked, and in reply the new dog trotted up and sniffed his bottom. Ellen laughed, then turned to watch as the two dogs chased each other about on the grass.

She was startled by a voice from behind her.

"Didn't you bring a towel? I'm soaking."

Ellen spun round and there, standing up to her knees in water, was Mirror-Belle. She had a dog lead in her hand and wore a stripy dress just like Ellen's, except that it was dripping wet.

"Mirror-Belle! What are you doing here? I thought you only came out of mirrors!" said Ellen. "Though I suppose the lake *is* a kind of mirror."

"We've been diving for treasure," replied Mirror-Belle.

Ellen was puzzled at first. Why had Mirror-Belle said "we" instead of "I"? But then the new dog bounded up to Mirror-Belle, nearly knocking her over. With his paws on her chest, he started to lick her face.

"I didn't know you had a dog too," said Ellen.

"Yes," said Mirror-Belle, in between licks. "His name is Prince Precious Paws."

Ellen thought this was rather a silly name but she was too polite to say so. "He looks just like my dog, Splodge," she said. "Does he like fetching sticks too?"

"Certainly not," said Mirror-Belle, as if she had never heard of such a thing. "Why would he want to fetch sticks when he can find rubies and emeralds?"

"Can he really?"

"Of course. How else do you suppose he helped the little tailor to seek his fortune?"

"What are you talking about? What little tailor? I thought you said he was your dog," said Ellen.

Before Mirror-Belle could launch into an explanation, Splodge – keen for more action and less talk – dropped a new stick at Ellen's feet. She was about to pick it up when Prince Precious Paws seized it and growled.

"You told me he didn't like sticks," said Ellen. She looked accusingly at Mirror-Belle, and Splodge looked accusingly at Prince Precious Paws.

Just then a woman with a pushchair came up to Mirror-Belle.

"You poor thing, did you fall in?" she asked. "I hope your twin sister didn't push you!"

"Ellen's not my twin," said Mirror-Belle indignantly. "I'm a princess and she's just an ordinary girl."

"There's a towel in here somewhere," said

the woman, rummaging in a bag. "William was going to go paddling but now he's fallen asleep in the pushchair."

As she took out the towel, a ball fell from the bag and rolled towards the water. Both dogs went after it, but Ellen called Splodge back.

"Come, Splodge! Sit!" she said, and Splodge came back obediently and sat at her feet.

Mirror-Belle's dog, however, seized the ball and started chewing it savagely, as if it was a rat he was trying to kill.

"Can you make him bring it back, please?" said the woman. "That's William's new ball and he'd be upset if your dog punctured it."

"I'm surprised you let your child play

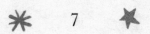

with such a flimsy toy," said Mirror-Belle. "Personally, I only ever play with a golden ball."

"Just call him back, will you?" said the woman impatiently.

"Very well." Mirror-Belle raised her voice. "Come, Prince Precious Paws, come!" she cried.

But Prince Precious Paws only growled and rested a paw on the ball.

"He's not very obedient, is he?" said the woman.

"Yes, he is – he's just a bit deaf," said Mirror-Belle. "You see, the tailor who owned him had two other dogs as well. These other two had such terribly loud barks that poor Prince Precious Paws's hearing was affected. So when I said

'Come', he probably thought I was saying 'Hum', and that's why he's making that noise."

As if in agreement, Prince Precious Paws began to growl even louder. It was a fierce sound, not like a hum at all, Ellen thought.

"I've never heard such nonsense," said the woman. "Look! Now he's ripping poor William's ball apart. I really think you should take him to dog-training classes. Your other dog seems to be very well trained. Are they from the same litter?"

"Of course not," said Mirror-Belle. "Prince Precious Paws is a royal dog. He lives in

a kennel lined with diamonds and pearls. Shall I tell you how he came to be mine?"

"No, thank you," said the woman. "I'm going to take William home before he wakes up and makes a fuss." And, snatching her towel back from Mirror-Belle, she strode off angrily.

Ellen felt embarrassed, and sorry for William, though she supposed that his mother would buy him a new ball. She thought about scolding Mirror-Belle, but perhaps it wasn't her fault that Prince Precious Paws was so badly behaved. Probably his previous owner hadn't brought him up properly.

"You can tell *me* if you like," she said, sitting down on a log by the lake. "How you got your dog, I mean."

Mirror-Belle sat down beside Ellen. Her dress and hair were already much drier, thanks to the hot sun and the woman's towel.

"Prince Precious Paws used to belong to a poor old woman," she began.

"I thought you said he belonged to a little tailor."

"That was later. The little tailor didn't have any dogs to start off with. All he had was a bit of bread and cheese in a red spotty handkerchief. He was seeking his fortune, you see. But then he met the poor old woman and gave her some of the bread and cheese, and in return for his kindness she gave him three dogs. They all had eyes as big as saucers."

"Are you sure?" asked Ellen.

She couldn't actually see Prince Precious Paws's eyes at that moment, as he was bounding away from them across the grass, pursued by Splodge, but as far as she remembered they were no bigger than Splodge's eyes.

Mirror-Belle ignored the interruption. "Luckily for the tailor," she continued,

"the three dogs were all brilliant at finding treasure. They kept finding it, in taverns and caves and all sorts of places, and in the end the tailor arrived at the palace with a great sackful of treasure and asked to marry the King's daughter."

"That's you, isn't it?" said Ellen. "But you're much too young to get married."

"Exactly," said Mirror-Belle. "So I said I'd take one of the dogs instead."

"What happened to the tailor?" asked Ellen, but she didn't find out, because at that moment they heard some angry shouting and saw Prince Precious Paws bounding towards them with something in his mouth. Behind him ran several people, including a man with glasses and a camera who looked vaguely familiar.

Ellen was relieved to see that her own dog was no longer with Prince Precious Paws but was scrabbling about under a nearby tree, probably looking for yet another stick.

"I'll just see what Splodge is up to," she said, and – feeling rather cowardly – she left Mirror-Belle to face the angry people on her own.

"Your dog's stolen our roast chicken!" she heard the man with the camera complain, and suddenly Ellen recognized him. He was Mr Spalding, a science teacher at her brother Luke's school. Mr Spalding ran a Saturday nature-study club called the Sat Nats. The club was open to adults and teenagers. A couple of the keener members of Luke's class – the ones he called the "geeks" – were members, but Luke himself preferred lying in bed on Saturday mornings.

The other Sat Nats were joining in with Mr Spalding now.

"He knocked over the lemonade."

"He's ruined our picnic."

"I don't call that much of a picnic," replied Mirror-Belle. "One measly roast chicken and a bottle of lemonade! I can assure you, Prince Precious Paws is used to far grander picnics than that. He was probably expecting roast swan and champagne."

A couple of the Sat Nats laughed at this, but not Mr Spalding. "Make him drop the chicken," he ordered.

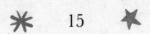

To Ellen's surprise, Mirror-Belle did say, "Drop it, Prince Precious Paws," in a commanding voice, but Prince Precious Paws took no notice and just started swinging the chicken from side to side.

"He's rather deaf, poor creature," Mirror-Belle explained. "He probably thought I said 'rock it'."

This just made Mr Spalding even angrier. He took a photograph of Prince Precious Paws with the chicken and said he would show it to Mirror-Belle's parents. "Where do you live?" he asked her.

"In the palace, of course," she replied, "and I very much doubt if the guards would let you in. You don't exactly look like royalty. Oh, and whatever you do, don't try picnicking in the palace grounds.

That's strictly forbidden."

"I know where she lives, sir," chipped in a teenage Sat Nat. "She's Luke Page's little sister."

Ellen's heart sank.

"I am no one of the sort," Mirror-Belle objected, but Mr Spalding seemed satisfied.

He led the Sat Nats back to the remains of their picnic.

"What an impertinent little man," remarked Princess Mirror-Belle, joining Ellen under the tree.

Ellen knew it would be useless to point out who had actually been the impertinent one. Instead, she fastened Splodge's lead to his collar. "I think

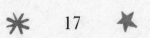

I'd better take him home now," she said.

"But we haven't found any treasure yet," protested Mirror-Belle. "I'm convinced that Prince Precious Paws is on the brink of a major discovery."

"Where is he?" asked Ellen.

They both looked around, but Mirror-Belle's dog was nowhere in sight.

"He's lost!" cried Mirror-Belle. "What a catastrophe! I shall have to offer a reward to whoever finds him. Do you think a chest of gold would be enough, or should I offer half my father's kingdom?"

"Why don't we just look for him ourselves?" said Ellen. "He can't have gone far. Let's walk round the lake and call him."

So that is what they did, although Ellen half wished she hadn't suggested it, because she felt so stupid calling out "Prince Precious Paws!" time after time.

"Can't we just call 'Prince'?" she suggested to Mirror-Belle.

"Absolutely not. Prince Precious Paws would never answer to such a common name. In fact, he'd probably run a mile in the other direction."

In the end it was Splodge who picked up the scent. He led the two girls away from the lake along a path which took them over a stile and into a field.

"Oh, no," said Ellen. "We're out of the park now. This is a farm. I hope your dog doesn't chase sheep."

"Only if they're wolves in disguise," said Mirror-Belle, which didn't make Ellen feel much better.

In fact, there were no farm animals in the field, but as they crossed it Ellen heard a loud bleating chorus coming from over the hedge.  They climbed another stile and there, huddled in a corner of the next field, was a flock of terrified-looking sheep. Barking as loudly as the sheep were bleating, and making little runs at them, was Prince Precious Paws.

Splodge pulled on the lead and barked. Prince Precious Paws turned and – almost as if to say, "Your turn now"– bounded away into yet another field.

"I hope we don't meet the farmer," said Ellen, keeping Splodge tightly on the lead as they followed Prince Precious Paws. When they caught up with him, he was barking down a hole in a bank of earth.

"It's probably the entrance to an underground cave full of priceless jewels," said Mirror-Belle.

Ellen thought it looked more like the entrance to a rabbit warren, but you never knew. Prince Precious Paws seemed very excited. His tail was wagging and his precious paws were scrabbling away in the earth. Now his head was half inside the hole and he seemed to be tugging at something.

"It could be the handle of a treasure chest," said Mirror-Belle.

"Or maybe some Roman remains," suggested Ellen, growing quite excited herself. "Luke went on a dig near here once and found part of an ancient vase with pictures of dancers on it."

Just then, Prince Precious Paws growled and his head emerged from the hole. He shook the earth from the object in his jaws. It wasn't a treasure chest or a Roman vase.

"It's a dirty old sheep's skull," said Ellen.

"Oh, good," said Mirror-Belle.

"What's so good about it?"

Mirror-Belle thought for a moment and then said, "Haven't

you heard of the legendary sheep with the golden fleece? Its bones are obviously buried here. That means that the golden fleece itself must be nearby – probably hanging from a tree and guarded by a fierce dragon. Prince Precious Paws will find it soon – just wait and see."

"I'm afraid I can't," said Ellen. "I've got to go home for lunch." She had spotted a gate leading to the road that would take her back home.

"I'll catch up with you as soon as we've found the golden fleece," said Mirror-Belle, though Ellen rather hoped she wouldn't.

Ellen was just setting off down the road with Splodge when a voice stopped her in her tracks.

"It's that dog again!"

She peeped over the hedge and saw Mr Spalding climbing over the stile into the field, followed by his troop of poor hungry Sat Nats.

"He's still not on the lead!"

"What's that he's got?"

"It's a sheep's skull, isn't it, Mr Spalding? He must have killed one of the sheep and eaten it!"

Ellen didn't stop to hear more, but hurried on with Splodge. It was quite a long walk and she was going to be late for lunch. They were just coming to the place where the road bent sharply and led towards the village when she heard footsteps. She turned and saw Mirror-Belle running towards her. Prince Precious Paws was on the lead at last, and was tugging her along at an amazing speed.

"Can't stop, must fly," Mirror-Belle greeted Ellen as they overtook her and went careering round the bend.

"Watch out, that's a dangerous corner!" Ellen called after them.

When she and Splodge rounded the same bend a minute later, there was no sign of Mirror-Belle or her dog. Although they'd been going so fast, Ellen hadn't expected them to be out of sight already. But then she noticed the mirror by the roadside. It was there so that drivers could see what was coming round the corner. Mirror-Belle and Prince Precious Paws must have disappeared into it.

The next day, Luke was practising his electric guitar in his bedroom when the doorbell rang. No one else seemed to be in, so reluctantly he went to the door and was surprised to see his science teacher standing outside.

"Good afternoon, Luke. Are either of your parents in?"

"No, they're not," said Luke, feeling suddenly guilty, as if his teacher somehow knew he hadn't started on his science homework yet.

"Don't worry, this isn't about school," said Mr Spalding, and Luke relaxed a little. He guessed that his teacher must be trying to recruit new members for the Sat Nats.

"I'd really like to join your club, Mr Spalding, but I'm usually rather busy on Saturday mornings, doing my homework, and . . . er . . . taking the dog for a walk."

Hearing his favourite word, Splodge appeared in the hallway, his lead in his mouth.

"Here's the culprit himself," said Mr Spalding. "That dog is badly in need of training."

Luke started to protest, but Mr Spalding reached into his pocket and handed him two photographs.

"Stealing food and running about off the lead on a sheep farm. Would you call that the behaviour of a well-trained dog?"

Luke studied the photographs. One showed a brown-and-white dog with what looked like a roast chicken in his jaws. In the other picture, the same dog was proudly resting his paw on a sheep skull.

Luke frowned, but then his face cleared.

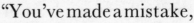

"You've made a mistake, Mr Spalding. You see, we call our dog Splodge because of the brown splodges on

his side and over his eye."

"Exactly. And there they are in the pictures – there's no denying it."

"But Splodge's marks are on his right side and over his right eye – look, you can see. This dog's marks are on his left side and over his left eye."

Mr Spalding looked from the photographs to Splodge and back again. "You're quite right . . . But the girl he was with looked just like your sister . . . It's most extraordinary."

"Don't worry, Mr Spalding. We all make mistakes sometimes," said Luke graciously.

"Well, I do apologize. And perhaps I should apologize to you, old chap," said Mr Spalding, patting Splodge rather timidly on the head.

Luke wondered if Splodge knew he had been wrongly accused. Maybe he even knew who the mystery dog was. But Splodge just gazed up at Mr Spalding with his usual trusting expression. Whatever he knew, he was keeping quiet about it.

Chapter Two

Which Witch?

"Two witches flew out on a moonlit
  night.
Their laughs were loud and their eyes
  were bright.
Their chins and their noses were
  pointed and long.
They shared the same broom and they
  sang the same song.
Their hats and their cloaks were as
  black as pitch,

And nobody knew which witch was
    which."

It was Halloween. Ellen, dressed up as a
witch, was practising the poem she was
planning to go round reciting with her
friend Katy.

Most of Ellen's other friends
were going out trick-or-
treating, but Ellen's mum
disapproved of that. She
said that in Scotland, where
she grew up, children had
to recite a poem or tell
a joke to earn their
Halloween treats. So
that was what Ellen
and Katy were going

to do. It was called guising.

Downstairs, Mum was teaching the piano. One of her star pupils was playing a fast piece whose tune kept going very low and then very high. It reminded Ellen of a witch swooping and soaring on her broomstick, and made her feel excited.

The phone rang. Ellen answered it, and a snuffly Katy said, "It's so unfair. My mum won't let me go out, just because my cold's got worse."

"Oh, poor you," said Ellen, but it was herself she really felt sorry for. As she put the phone down, all her excitement vanished. What was she going to do? She didn't feel like going out on her own, and anyway the poem was supposed to be recited by two identical witches. But

✳ 35 ✵

now it was too late to ask anyone else to go with her. She would just have to stay at home. What a waste of all the trouble she had taken over her costume – sewing silver stars on to the cloak, spraying glitter on the hat and carving a face out of her pumpkin lantern. She glanced wistfully at herself in the mirror.

"What's the matter? Don't tell me you've lost your cat," came a familiar voice, and a witchy Princess Mirror-Belle stepped out of the mirror, shedding glitter and flourishing her wand.

For once, Ellen was delighted to see her. "What good timing!" she greeted Mirror-Belle. "Now we can go guising together!"

"Disguising is not for the likes of me," said Mirror-Belle. "Your costume may be a disguise, but I really *am* a witch."

"I said *guising*, not disguising," said Ellen, "and anyway, how can you be a witch when you're always telling me you're a princess?"

"Of course I'm a princess," replied Mirror-Belle. "But a wicked ogre has turned me into a witch. A *royal* witch, of course," she added hastily.

"Why did he do that?"

"Because my golden ball landed in his garden and he saw me climbing over his wall to get it back."

"If you're a real witch, can you actually fly

that broomstick?" asked Ellen hopefully. Mirror-Belle was holding a small twiggy broomstick just the same as her own.

"Unfortunately, the rotten wizard refused to give me a cat, and everyone knows that a broomstick won't fly without a cat on it. I was hoping that I could borrow your cat, but you seem to have let it escape."

"I never had one," said Ellen. "Anyway, Mirror-Belle, do please come guising with me. I'll teach you the poem, and then we can go round the houses and people will give us lots of goodies."

Mirror-Belle's eyes lit up at the mention of goodies and, after a quick rehearsal of the poem, she followed Ellen downstairs. The impressive sounds of Mum's star pupil were still drifting out of the sitting room.

Ellen found them each a carrier bag. "These are to collect the goodies," she explained. "Mum says we're only to go to people we know and only in this block."

They stepped out into the night.

"Let's start here," said Mirror-Belle, marching up to the house next door.

"No, number 17's been empty since the Johnsons moved out," Ellen told her. "We'll go to the Elliots'."

Mr and Mrs Elliot were the elderly couple who lived two doors along and always had a supply of old-fashioned sweets like pear drops and humbugs and bullseyes.

Mrs Elliot opened the door. She pretended to be scared. "Oh, help! I'd better let you in quickly, before you turn me into a toad," she said.

"Yes, that would be a good idea," Mirror-Belle agreed.

Mrs Elliot showed them into the cosy front room, where her husband was sitting in an armchair by the fire.

Ellen and Mirror-Belle recited their poem, and Ellen was pleased at how well Mirror-Belle remembered it.

"And nobody knew which witch was which," they finished up. At least, it was supposed to be the end, but Mirror-Belle carried on with another two lines:

"But one of the two was in fancy dress
    While the other was really a royal
        princess."

Mr Elliot chuckled, and Mrs Elliot said,
"You've definitely earned your bullseyes."

"I'd rather have some newts'
eyes, if you don't mind," said
Mirror-Belle. "They're better for
spells."

Mrs Elliot just laughed. She took
    down a big glass jar from the
        mantelpiece and began to pour
        some of the striped sweets into
        Mirror-Belle's carrier bag.
        "These don't look like eyes to
    me," Mirror-Belle complained.
"They're just boiled sweets. How are we

supposed to do any magic with them?"

Ellen glared at her, but the Elliots laughed again, as if Mirror-Belle had been performing another party piece.

Mr Elliot beckoned them over and handed them two fifty-pence pieces.

"Oh, I see," said Mirror-Belle. "You're expecting us to go to the eye shop ourselves." Then she studied her coin. "I don't think any decent eye shop would accept this," she said. "The writing is back to front."

"Stop being so cheeky," Ellen muttered, but Mr Elliot roared with laughter and said, "This beats the telly any day."

When they were back outside, Ellen ticked Mirror-Belle off again. "I know the Elliots thought it was funny, but other people might not," she said. "And I don't want to get Katy into trouble. Remember that people probably think you're her."

"But it's so puzzling," said Mirror-Belle. "What do witches want with sweets and money? Surely we should be collecting things like frogs' legs and vampires' teeth?" Then a thoughtful look crossed her face. "Oh, I understand," she said. "Well, we'd better get a move on. We're going to need a huge amount of sweets."

Ellen didn't really see why, but she wasn't in the mood for listening to a long, fanciful explanation, so she was relieved to see Mirror-Belle striding up the path of the next house and ringing on the bell.

An hour or so later, their carrier bags were full of sweets, biscuits, fruit and money.

"Shall we go back to my house?" Ellen suggested to Mirror-Belle, who had been remarkably well behaved — apart from adding the extra two lines to the poem every time they recited it.

"I don't think we'll need to do that," said Mirror-Belle mysteriously.

Before Ellen could ask what she meant, she was striding off again.

"Where are you going?" asked Ellen, trying to catch up.

"In here," said Mirror-Belle, and

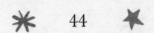

pointed her wand at the doors of the mini-supermarket at the end of the road. The doors swung open, as they always did, but she turned and gave Ellen a triumphant look as if she had performed some magic.

Mirror-Belle took a trolley. She dumped her wand and broomstick in it and hung her lantern and carrier bag on the hook at the back. Then she pushed it swiftly up the first aisle to the meat counter at the far end of the shop. Ellen had a horrible feeling that she was going

to start demanding newts' eyes and frogs' legs, but instead Mirror-Belle turned her back on the counter and began to recite the poem at the top of her voice.

There weren't many customers in the shop and, to Ellen's relief, no one took much notice. But her relief faded when Mirror-Belle, having finished her version of the poem on a note of triumph, pushed her trolley down the next aisle and started

filling it with sweets.

"You can't just take all of those!" Ellen protested, as Mirror-Belle threw in a dozen bags of toffees.

"I agree it would

have been polite of someone to offer them to us – not to mention loading the trolley – but unfortunately there's not a servant in sight," said Mirror-Belle, emptying the shelves of liquorice allsorts and reaching for the jelly babies. "It would be quicker if you'd help me," she added.

Ellen tried to think of something to say that would stop Mirror-Belle, but she knew from experience how difficult this was. In any case, the trolley was nearly full now and Mirror-Belle seemed satisfied with her haul.

"Come on," she said, and made her way to one of the checkouts. But instead of stopping and taking the sweets out, she sailed on through.

"Stop!" cried Ellen.

Mirror-Belle was about to push the trolley outside when a shop assistant ran after her and grabbed it.

Ellen felt terrified. What if they were both arrested for shoplifting?

"You haven't paid for this lot, have you?" said the assistant.

"Certainly not," replied Mirror-Belle. "Has it escaped your attention that this is Halloween and that Ellen and I are guising?"

"Not in here, you're not," the shop assistant said firmly.

Mirror-Belle turned to Ellen. "Shall we turn this rude servant into a black beetle?" she suggested.

The shop assistant ignored her and steered

the trolley firmly back to the checkout.

"You either pay for them or put them back," he said.

"It's extremely lucky for you that my wand is buried under all the sweets," Mirror-Belle told him. "Poor Ellen here  isn't a real witch like me, so she can't do the black-beetle spell."

Ellen could see that Mirror-Belle was just making the assistant angrier and she was scared that he might phone the police. She had to make Mirror-Belle see sense!

"Listen, Mirror-Belle," she said. "We did collect quite a lot of money. If you're so keen for more sweets, perhaps we can buy some of them."

Mirror-Belle sighed. "Very well," she

said, "if you think it will stop the servants rioting."

They had enough money for five bags of toffees, four each of liquorice allsorts and jelly babies, and six packets of chewing gum.

"But we'll be sick if we eat all these as well as the sweets and chocolates people gave us," Ellen objected as they left the shop.

"Eat them, did you say? *Eat* them?" Mirror-Belle laughed, as if the idea were absurd. "Where would we live if we ate them?"

"What are you talking about?"

"I'm afraid you're not very well informed about witches, Ellen. Didn't you know that they always live in houses made of sweets?"

Ellen thought about this. "I know that the witch in 'Hansel and Gretel' had a house of sweets – or was it gingerbread? – but I can't think of any others."

"Where will we build it, I wonder," mused Mirror-Belle, ignoring Ellen and marching back the way they had come. "I know! In the garden of that empty house."

"Mirror-Belle, don't be silly. We haven't got nearly enough sweets to build a house. And anyway, how would we stick them all together?"

"Chewing gum!" said Mirror-Belle, popping a piece into her mouth. "Ah, here we are."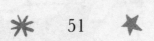

They had reached the empty house, and she opened the tall side gate which led into the overgrown back garden. Ellen followed her nervously.

"Oh, how thoughtful of somebody," said Mirror-Belle, pointing at a large shed in the corner of the garden. "Someone's built it for us already. We'll only need to decorate it."

At first Ellen just watched as Mirror-Belle started to stick jelly babies round one of the shed windows. But it did look rather good fun and soon she was joining in.

"Black, white, pink, yellow," she muttered, as she created a coloured pattern with liquorice allsorts round the other window. She was standing back to admire the effect when the garden gate creaked and began to open.

"Someone's coming!" she hissed. She pulled Mirror-Belle behind the shed, but couldn't stop her peeping round the edge.

"I think it's the delivery men, come to furnish our new house," said Mirror-Belle. "But surely we don't need two televisions?"

She hadn't lowered her voice, but luckily it was drowned by a crash and a curse from the garden.

Ellen couldn't resist a peep herself.

Although the garden was dark, she could make out two men, one carrying a television and another picking up a second television from the ground. Both of them were wearing balaclava helmets over their heads, so that only their eyes showed. They didn't look like delivery men to Ellen, more like burglars who were hiding stolen goods. But she didn't risk whispering this fear to Mirror-Belle, in case they heard her.

One of the men had opened the shed door and must have been putting the televisions inside, while the other went back through the gate and then reappeared with a large square object covered in a sheet. Probably a stolen picture, thought Ellen.

A sudden idea struck her. If she and

Mirror-Belle climbed over the low wall into her own garden, they could get into her house through the back door and phone the police. With a finger over her lips, she pointed at the wall and then beckoned to Mirror-Belle.

Ellen was already over the wall when she realized that Mirror-Belle wasn't following her.

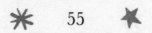

"It's a witch!" she heard one of the men say, and, "Don't be daft, it's a kid," from the other. And then came Mirror-Belle's voice – loud, clear and bossy as ever: "Don't just dump that on the floor. Aren't you going to hang it on the wall?"

Instead of following Ellen, Mirror-Belle must have gone to check what sort of a job the "delivery men" were doing.

Ellen stood frozen, uncertain whether to join Mirror-Belle or run home for help. Then she heard one of the men again. This time he was talking to Mirror-Belle.

"I do apologize, madam. Just step inside and wait while we fetch our toolbox."

The next sounds came quickly. A slam, a metallic clink, some bashing and an angry "Let me out! What is the meaning of this?" from Mirror-Belle. Then footsteps and the creak of the garden gate. The men had locked Mirror-Belle in the shed and escaped!

But *had* they both escaped? Ellen didn't dare investigate by herself. Instead, she ran through her own garden and into the house through the back door.

"Help! Help!" she cried.

Dad came out of the kitchen, followed by Mum and Luke.

"What's the matter? Did a skeleton jump out at you?" Dad asked jokily.

"The burglars have locked Mirror-Belle in the shed next door!" shrieked Ellen.

"And now they're getting away!"

Mum and Dad still seemed to think this was some Halloween prank. It was Luke who ran to the front window.

"Two men are getting into a van," he reported. "And they're wearing masks, or hoods, or something."

"Take down the number," said Dad, and reached for the phone to call the police.

Mum made Ellen sit down and drink

some hot sweet tea "for shock".

When Ellen protested, "But we must go back next door! Mirror-Belle's trapped! We've got to rescue her!" Dad said, "Not till the police arrive." Ellen knew he thought Mirror-Belle was just an imaginary friend.

"Where's Katy?" said Mum suddenly.

"She's all right. She's at home," said Ellen, but Mum phoned Katy's parents just the same.

"That's strange. She's in bed with a cold," Mum said, sounding relieved but puzzled.

"Yes . . . she couldn't come, but then Mirror-Belle . . ." Ellen began, but a ring at the bell interrupted her explanation. It was the police.

*

Katy was back at school on Monday. Like the rest of Ellen's class, she had read in the paper about Ellen's discovery of the shed full of stolen goods, and of how the burglars had been caught thanks to Luke getting the number of their van.

"Just think! If only I hadn't had that cold I'd be in the paper too," she said.

"But if you'd come with me instead of Mirror-Belle, we wouldn't have gone to number 17."

"Did the police find Mirror-Belle as well as all the televisions?" asked Katy. Unlike Ellen's family, she believed in Mirror-Belle, who had once come to their school.

"No," said Ellen. "You see, the men hadn't just stolen televisions. When we were there they were hiding away

something else. I thought it was a great
big picture, but it wasn't."

"What was it, then?" asked Katy.

"It was a mirror," said Ellen.

Chapter Three

The Princess Test

"I hope you haven't put spaghetti on that shopping list," said Ellen to her brother, Luke. "Or mince. Or tinned tomatoes."

"Don't worry, bossyboots, we're not going to have spag bol again." Luke crumpled the shopping list and stuffed it into his pocket. "I'm going to make chicken vindaloo."

"What's that?"

"It's this really hot curry."

Ellen wasn't sure that really hot curry would be the right sort of supper for Mum, who had just had her appendix out. But it was a relief that it wouldn't be yet more spaghetti bolognese, which was what Dad had cooked just about every night of the week Mum had been in hospital. It used to be Ellen's favourite food, but now she didn't mind if she never ate it again.

Mum was coming home today; Dad had gone to fetch her from the hospital. He had warned Ellen and Luke that she would still be a bit weak after the operation and that they would have to be extra helpful. So Luke had agreed to do the shopping and cook the supper, and Ellen was going to make the bedroom look nice for Mum's return.

Luke went out, slamming the front door, and Ellen took the cleaning things upstairs. She had decided to make Mum a "Welcome Home" card and pick some flowers from the garden. But first she really ought to do the boring housework-y things.

She straightened the duvet on the bed and then picked up the yellow duster.

Dust was such funny stuff, she thought to herself. No one actually sprinkled it on the furniture; it just appeared from nowhere. "And what *is* it exactly?" she wondered out loud as she began to dust Mum's dressing table.

"What is what?" came a voice.

"Dust," Ellen replied automatically, and then, "Mirror-Belle! It's you!"

"Yes, though why you should be asking me questions about dust I have no idea.

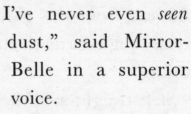

I've never even *seen* dust," said Mirror-Belle in a superior voice.

There were three mirrors on Mum's dressing table: a big one in the middle and, joined on to it, two smaller ones

which slanted inwards. Mirror-Belle was leaning out of the middle mirror. "You seem to forget that I'm a princess, not a maid," she said.

"Oh, no, you're not," came another voice, and Ellen was amazed to see a second Mirror-Belle – at least, that was what she looked like – sticking a hand out of the left-hand mirror and wagging a finger at the first Mirror-Belle. "You know very well that you're a maid. You're *my* maid." She turned to Ellen

and said, "She's always disguising herself as me. Once, when we were on a journey to another kingdom, she made me swap clothes and horses with her, and when we got there she managed to kid everyone that she was the princess, so I was sent to feed the geese."

"What a pack of lies," said the first Mirror-Belle, who had slithered out of the mirror and was swinging her legs to the ground. "She's got it the wrong way round. *She's* the maid and *I'm* the one who had to feed the geese. But of course my sweet singing soon made everyone realize that I was the real princess."

"You've got a voice like a crow," said the second Mirror-Belle, beginning to slither out herself.

The first one tried to push her back, and Ellen cried, "Be careful or you'll break the glass!"

"Stop this commotion at once!" came another voice. A third identical girl was reaching out from the right-hand mirror and had picked up Mum's silver-backed hairbrush. "Now, you two lazybones, whose turn is it to brush my hair today?"

"Are *you* the real Mirror-Belle?" asked Ellen.

"Naturally – don't you recognize me?" said the newest Mirror-Belle, but the other two said, "Nonsense," and, "She's Ethel, the kitchen maid."

"Well, you all look exactly the same to me," said Ellen. "And none of you looks specially like a princess. You don't really look like maids either. At least, I suppose you have all got dusters, but you haven't got caps and aprons. Really, you all look just like me."

All three Mirror-Belles had a complicated explanation for this, but since they all talked at once Ellen couldn't make out what the different explanations were, and she didn't really care.

"I give up," she said. "In any case, does it really matter who's who?"

"Of course it does!" said all three mirror girls together.

This at least was something they were agreed on.

"I know!" said the first one. "You must give us a test, Ellen, to find out which is the true princess."

"What sort of a test?" Ellen asked.

"Well, if you had a frog, you could see which of us could kiss it and turn it into a prince," said the second girl.

"Or we could lie on the bed and see who could detect if there was a pea under the mattress," suggested the third one. "Only a real princess could do that."

"I haven't got a frog," said Ellen, "and I've only just made the bed. I don't want you all messing it up again." In any case, she had bad memories of pea-detection and frog-kissing. Mirror-Belle had tried these things out in a shop once and got them both into trouble.

Still, Ellen quite liked the idea of a test.

"I'll think of something," she told them. "But first, I must be able to tell you apart. Just stand still a minute."

She took one of Mum's lipsticks from a little drawer in the dressing table. She wrote a big L on the forehead of the

Mirror-Belle who had come out of the left mirror. On the foreheads of the other two she wrote R and M, for right and middle.

"What is the test going to be?" they all kept clamouring.

"It's a quiz," said Ellen, "and I'm the quizmaster."

She was enjoying herself. For once she was the one in charge, instead of being ordered about by Mirror-Belle. But it was going to be hard thinking up the questions.

"I'll just put Mum's lipstick back in the drawer," she said, and that made her wonder what a princess would call her own mother. She wouldn't say "Mum", like an ordinary person, surely? But "Your Majesty" didn't sound quite right either. This was something that a real princess would know the answer to, and would

make a good quiz question.

"Question number one: what do you call your mother?"

They all answered at once, so Ellen made them take turns.

"Your Mumjesty," said Mirror-Belle L.

"Queen Mother," said Mirror-Belle R.

"O Most Royal Madam whom I Respect and Obey without Question," said Mirror-Belle M.

Ellen couldn't decide which of these sounded right, so she moved on to another question. A dog barking in the distance made her think about Mirror-Belle's dog, Prince Precious Paws, and that gave her another idea.

"What would a real princess give to her dog for his birthday?" she asked.

This time she made them answer in a different order.

"A golden bone," said Mirror-Belle R.

"How common! An emerald-studded collar would be a far more suitable gift," said Mirror-Belle M.

"What's so special about that?" asked Mirror-Belle L. "I'm planning to give Prince Precious Paws something magical – an invisible lead, which will make *him* invisible when I put it on him. In fact, I've brought one for your dog, Splodge, too. Here it is." She reached out to Ellen as if she were handing her something.

The other two Mirror-Belles became very indignant at this.

"She's an impostor!" cried Mirror-Belle R. "Besides, I've brought you a *far* better invisible present. It's . . . um . . . a spoon that will change whatever you're eating into your favourite food."

Ellen didn't really believe in the invisible spoon, but she pretended to take it and said, "I wish I'd had this when Dad was doing the cooking."

"Invisible spoons are two a penny," said Mirror-Belle M scornfully. "I've brought you . . . er . . . some invisible pyjamas. If you wear them at night, all your dreams will come true."

All three Mirror-Belles were crowding

round her, offering her more and more invisible things, and Ellen was losing the feeling of being the one in charge. The quiz seemed to have turned into a boasting session.

"And here's an invisible clock . . ." began Mirror-Belle M.

"Stop!" cried Ellen.

The invisible clock had reminded her that Mum would be back from hospital soon. She would never get the bedroom ready at this rate. Not on her own, anyway, and the three Mirror-

78

Belles were so eager to prove that they were not maids they would never agree to help. Unless . . .

Suddenly, Ellen had an idea. "I've thought of a test," she said. "I've just remembered that there is a . . . a sort of fairy imprisoned in the furniture in this room and only a true princess will be able to set her free."

The Mirror-Belles started opening drawers, but Ellen stopped them.

"No, the fairy's not in a drawer or cupboard. She's in the actual *wood* of the furniture. You have to rub the wood to get her out."

"Oh, a wood nymph, you mean," said Mirror-Belle R. "Why didn't you say so before?" and she immediately began to rub the dressing table with her duster.

"She might be in the mantelpiece . . . or in the wood of the bedside table," suggested Ellen, and the other two Mirror-Belles set to work with their dusters.

They were all rubbing furiously. Soon there was not a speck of dust to be seen, and the furniture was shiny bright.

"You've all failed that test," Ellen said. "The wood nymph doesn't seem to realize that one of you is a princess."

Once again, all

three Mirror-Belles
started on
explanations
for this,
but Ellen
interrupted
them. "I've
thought of a
different test,"

she said. "Well, it's more of a quest than a
test. Down in the garden there is a talking
flower. But it will only talk if it's picked
and put into a vase of water by a true
princess."

The three girls ran to the bedroom
door, eager to be downstairs and out in
the garden. Ellen was suddenly afraid
that they would pick every single flower,

so she called out after them, "The flower will only talk if the princess picks no more than five flowers altogether."

While the Mirror-Belles picked the flowers, Ellen filled a vase with water and put it on Mum's gleaming bedside table. She was just making a start on her "Welcome Home" card when the Mirror-Belles charged back into the room and thrust their flowers into the vase. The flowers looked very pretty but they were completely silent.

"I expect the magic flower is too shy to talk to me when there are two maids in the room," said one of the Mirror-Belles, and the other two said, "To *me*, you mean."

Just then Ellen heard the front door bang. Help! Was Dad back with Mum already? The room did look really nice now, but how was she going to get rid of the three Mirror-Belles? She was sure Mum wouldn't want them all in her bedroom when she was trying to rest.

"I'm back!" came Luke's voice.

Of course – she should have recognized the way he slammed the door. Still, Mum would be back any minute now.

"Give us another test, Ellen," the Mirror-Belles were demanding, and suddenly Ellen knew what to do.

"All right," she said, "but this one is really difficult. You've given me all these invisible presents, which is very nice of you, but I'm sure that only a real princess would know how to make *herself* invisible."

As Ellen closed her eyes and counted to a hundred, she remembered the very first time she had ever met Mirror-Belle. That time, Mirror-Belle had tricked her by blindfolding her with toilet paper and then disappearing into the bathroom mirror. This time, it was Ellen who was tricking Mirror-Belle. She felt a bit guilty and wondered where she had learned to make up so many stories. But of course she knew the answer really – it was from Mirror-Belle.

As she had hoped, when she got to a hundred and opened her eyes, the room was empty. She was very careful indeed not to steal a glance at the mirrors on the dressing table, in case the mirror princesses (or maids) reappeared. Instead, she lay on her tummy on the floor and carried on with the "Welcome Home" card.

She had just finished it when she heard the front door opening again.

Ellen jumped to her feet and ran downstairs into the arms of the person she most wanted to see in the whole world.

"Come and look at your bedroom, Mum!" she said.

"Don't tire her out," said Dad, but Mum laughed and let herself be tugged upstairs by Ellen.

She admired the

card and the flowers and the neatly made bed. "And what shining surfaces!" she said. "I never knew you were so good at housework, Ellen! It's a real treat to come home to this."

Ellen wished that Mirror-Belle could hear. She was the one who deserved most of the praise.

"I wanted you to have a nice treat to come home to," she muttered to Mum.

Mum hugged her again and said, "Do you know what the biggest treat is? Seeing you!"

A strong spicy smell was wafting into the room.

"That smells even better than spaghetti bolognese," said Mum, and together they went downstairs.

Also available

For younger readers